1 Hold one end of the sari and tuck it into the slip to the right of the belly button.

2 Keep tucking all around the back to the front.

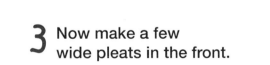

3 Now make a few
wide pleats in the front.

4 Tuck the pleats
into the slip.

Text copyright © 2006 by Sandhya Rao
Illustrations copyright © 2006 by Nina Sabnani.
First published in India by Tulika Publishers under the title *My Mother's Sari*.
New English edition copyright © 2006 by North-South Books Inc.

First published in the United States, Great Britain, Canada, Australia, and New Zealand in 2006 by North-South Books Inc., an imprint of NordSüd Verlag AG, Zürich, Switzerland.
First paperback edition published in 2009.
Distributed in the United States by North-South Books Inc., New York.

Library of Congress Cataloging-in-Publication Data is available.
A CIP catalogue record for this book is available from The British Library.

ISBN 978-0-7358-2101-9 (trade edition)
10 9 8 7 6 5 4 3 2

ISBN 978-0-7358-2233-7 (paperback)
10 9 8 7 6 5 4 3 2 1

Printed in China

My Mother's Sari

WRITTEN BY **Sandhya Rao** ILLUSTRATED BY **Nina Sabnani**

NorthSouth
New York / London

My mother's sari.

My mother's sari

is long like a train.

It fil

...e air with color
...hen I dance and sing.

I sail down a rive

and climb up a rope.

I hide with my friends.

I even wipe my nose.

Then, when I am tired,
it wraps itself around me.

I sleep while it gently swings
beneath a shady tree.

I love my mother's sari . . .

and how it makes me dream.

5 Gather the rest of the sari, take it around the waist and bring to the front.

6 Now take it across the chest and throw the end over the left shoulder.

7 Where did all that cloth go?

8 Now you know!